swallowed
a
twinkling
star

katja pesonen

CONTENTS

Winter

Red gloves like frozen
raspberries rising towards
the glistening sky.
I can reach the rim of it.
Yet I'm feeling limitless.

”It is possible
to have it all”, he says in
a strong, cottonsoft
voice. ”For I had you and will
lack nothing ever again.”

The drowsy touch that
wine brings. On the arch of a
back, on a shoulder.
Heat. You take off my sweater.
We're breathing at the same pace.

I'm sure nothing beats
your honeyrich voice when you
whisper how precious
I am to you and you want
to wake up with me always.

White musk. You smell like
it and it swallows me whole
like a sandstorm at
Coachella. It makes me
want to get naked right here.

Your tongue tastes my skin
with thirst, hunger and yearning.
Let it glide inside
where the fountain flows and the
heart of the Earth beats in wait.

This moment is real,
like a mountain, as I feel
a soul touching a
soul, hand, neck, eyes, lips, hips, back.
Beings intertwining as one.

You of all people
are making me dizzy like
a tipsy Tuesday
when the intoxication
wafts a light, sheer gossamer.

Moka pot whistling
in the morning mist and you're
toasting bread loudly.
Damn you morning people! Come
back to bed for a cuddle!

Beauty is not
in the eyes of the beholder,
but in his eyes when
he comes from the shower in
just a towel. Too much on.

Bed is an island
and the fireplace the Sun.
The humidity
of our skin could easily
melt a frosty white forest.

The wind can go now.
The snow is welcome to melt.
There cannot be more
moments where you are this far
from our homemade universe.

I'm on the carpet
streetlights illuminating
the room and my face.
It is cruel how long I am
forced to wait for your warm lips.

Shadows are flying
on the ceiling, depicting
doves as if they could
be bringing grave messages
of incipient longing.

Leafless basswoods and
car tracks sunken in the snow.
In the backyard I'm
making a snow angel and
watching the dark starry sky.

Spring

Can you come up with
just one reason to explain
why we couldn't walk
across the park hand in hand
so that everyone could see?

Your eyes aren't burning
through me anymore the way
they did before, at
the beginning of all things.
Your fragrance has drifted far.

If I put on a
red dress and caressed your thigh
like a lily, coy
and subtle, or passionate and
torrid, would you love me then?

”It doesn't serve you –
or anybody – to grab
the wind with both hands”, he said,
”as people like me should be
as free as eagles and fly.”

Your frozen lips are
telling me everything I
needed to know. I
grab my jacket and take the
next bus home in the dark rain.

Even if I had
revealed my true emotions
that dark night by the
fire, you'd still have chosen
differently. For you knew.

Frost has drawn your face
on the glass as if mocking
yesterday. I sigh
and it melts. I hope you are
melting with it, vanishing.

Like a stranger you
have been in my heart,
just a person dropping by.
You never meant to stay long.
You can leave. I'll close the door.

This flat is haunted
by ghosts born of emotions
killed in a war that
lasted so long, it feels like
life was totally wasted.

Crawling up into
a big ball of darkness in
my bedroom corner.
I long to escape this veil
of dwelling deep in the past.

Some days I want to
stop crying, others I want
to do only that.
Maybe I can just do both
until my tears diminish.

Love, deep connection.
No, I can't imagine that.
This time has made me
cold, bitter, closed and vanquished.
Can't find a way out of this.

I have no choice but
to jump over the edge of
my wounded soul, though
I can already taste the
blood in my throat from the fear.

They say that courage
is not the absence of fear
but to be scared yet
do it anyway. I want
to have the courage to trust.

You don't know and you
don't care that I'm starting to
forget. You are like
a prayer gone unanswered.
A see-through moment, so sheer.

Summer

How can I tell if
a green worm is living in
a green apple? How
can I know if the fruit is
not just rotten to the core?

I mean, can I trust
my ability to know
who is screwing me
physically and who's screwing
me mentally? I'm not sure.

A moon so bright it's
a guiding light to a man
rowing a boat and
retrieving fishing nets from
the lake. Quite calming to watch.

Even though it's dark
I'm dipping my feet into
the water, feeling
the little waves caressing
my toes. I'm ambling deeper.

Has the sun always
been so bright or did I just
spend too long in the
darkness? And have the bluebells
always been so blue? Funny.

Lilac is spreading
its sugary scent in the
wind. I'm eating an
avocado on the porch.
Soft white clouds are gliding by.

I'm everything, but
at the same time, I'm nothing.
My sigh and longing
are one. There's a sky inside.
I reach up to the sky's rim.

Picnic in the park.
Feels like I have swallowed a
twinkling star, my heart
is so light. I sit beside
a field of tiger lilies.

The morning breeze chirps
through an open window and
the rising sun makes
lace patterns through the curtains
onto the wall. Grateful still.

The grass is almost
always greener in places
that have been burned to
a cinder and reduced to
ashes. I will be the grass.

This land is enough
for someone but not for me.
I can't breathe at my
own pace and fly my own way.
I dare you to tie me down.

Before starting a
new relationship, your soul
must be almost healed.
No-one is going to fill the
void inside calling your name.

The void that you have
doesn't come from their leaving,
or being alone.
It comes from you leaving you.
Know that nothing is lacking.

Be on your own side.
You don't want to miss out on
life because someone
wronged you or did not see your
worth. Show *you* how wrong they were.

I think we are all
somehow a little bit lost.
So don't feel bad if
you don't have it all figured
out. Life isn't about stopping.

Autumn

When the sun and the
autumn wind coalesce, I
feel new life begin.
Leaves may die but trees do not.
They are plotting their rebirth.

A random woman
traipses through the pouring rain
under a hot pink
umbrella. She carries a
banana skin. How odd!

I put dried bluebells
in a vase, make a cup of
dark roasted coffee,
then drown myself in books and
blankets. The rain sound calms me.

Yellow leaves. The wind
whistles through them and it looks
like it's protecting
them from falling. I'm leaning
against the maple, dreaming.

Wild rivers grow from
wild thoughts that push their way through
rocks, cliffs and outcrops
with such power that they clear
roads for the brave to walk on.

When he looked at me
across a crowded street, my
world lost all reason.
Passing cars faded away.
I felt a deep warmth inside.

Overcrowded and
jammed traffic. Back of a hand
touching a lapel.
In that moment, everything
is so soundless and serene.

"Quite some traffic, huh?"
He said nervously and touched
the collar of his
coat. "Yes, many cars out there!"
My god, what did I just say?

He was standing there,
on a doorstep, soaking wet.
Without a gesture
he handed me a small bag
of cherries. I love cherries.

His fingertips are
running gently down my spine.
Erykah Badu's
creamy music plays in the
background, surrounds this moment.

Let's run together
through the midst of a thunder
storm. I can be your
umbrella, you can be my
rubber boots. Or let's just soak.

Today I'm riding
on a hill with him, under
a maple tree. We
roll among the fallen leaves
and moss like trolls, fauns and nymphs.

The stubble on his
wiry cheeks softly tickles
my smooth inner thighs.
The forest rocks us towards
another realm of being.

You are treating me
exactly the way that I
want. You don't even
know it. I can't believe you
really exist. In the flesh.

I wish I'd known that
all of my waiting would be
rewarded with this
kind of bliss, I'd have trusted
sooner that life has our back.

ABOUT THE AUTHOR

Katja Pesonen is a Finnish journalist who has studied Finnish language, creative writing and art history. Her first book Tangat was published 2018. It's a tanka poetry book in Finnish and Swallowed a twinkling star is an extended version of the book in English. She lives in Helsinki and is crazy about poetry and chocolate.